Minecraft House Ideas

70 Top Minecraft House Ideas Your Friends Wish They Know

Jason Scotts

Table of Contents

Jason Scotts

Building Material

The type of building material you will use for your house is pretty basic in Minecraft. It's actually one of the things you will have to think about when crafting and designing your houses. Some materials can be used to pimp up the place and some of them are there for functional purposes.

So, when you ask what materials are your favorites or what materials you often use to build your house, the answer usually varies from player to player. However, players will provide a certain caveat; that it all depends on the type of house or shelter you're building.

Two Main Reasons for Material Selection

The two main reasons for material selection are that the material is either to be used for aesthetic purposes (i.e. to make your shelter/house look nice). Who would want to live in a dump, right? Some houses are nice, your basic blocks in place but if it's plain and bland you might want to spice up the view and add some outrageous looking things to make it more interesting. Besides, it's also something that you can brag about to your friends in case you can pull it off.

The usual materials that everyone uses to build a basic shelter include wood and cobblestone. A good idea is to add a few combinations to your choice of materials. Some people might suggest the use of stone and bricks into the structure while others will just settle for stone bricks to keep the peace.

Another favorite material is glass; there are a good number of players who would opt for such materials. Well, basically glass allows you to see what's going on outside. You can then plan your next move since you already know who or what is waiting for you when you open the door. But just like any other material, glass also has its own downside.

Idea #1 – Use Basic Materials for Aesthetic Appeal

Some materials, even though they are functional in nature can have that aesthetic appeal. Materials like wood, glass, and stone bricks have their basic functions but they make the basic structure look really good. Some materials are flammable like wood and wooden planks but they also have their uses depending on the time of the day or the situation you're currently in.

Idea #2 – Use Contrasting Colors and Other Elements

Here's another interesting suggestion when it comes to choosing fundamental materials to pimp your crib. Sandstone by itself really looks good. A lot of players will call it unoriginal but it is a definite staple if you consider how many people use it when they construct their shelters. If you want to put some contrast to the elements in your walls then you can arrange sandstone, contrast it with redstone, and add a good amount of snow to complete the effect.

The way you implement building materials in your houses also creates this contrasting effect. For instance, glass is a material that can break while obsidian is often a material that people rely on for strength. Besides, obsidian is explosion proof, which is why everyone uses it to keep creepers out of the premises.

Other colorful and aesthetically sound materials that can be used include snow blocks, spruce wood, and lapis lazuli blocks. Brightly colored wood is also a good option in case you want to brighten up the mood in the interiors. You can use white wool and lace it over spruce logs; and another idea is to mix bricks and oak wood.

Remember that the mix of colors can brighten or dull the overall theme inside and outside your house.

Idea #3 – Use Materials for Their Functional Value

Another basic idea, something that everyone learns at the onset of the game is that there are materials that have functional uses. For some basic protection you should go for some blocks that are rather hard to break. Obsidian blocks easily come to mind since they are tougher but they are indeed a little tougher to work with. Everyone knows that each type of block has its own level of resistance to explosions.

Some of the other options for strength and stability include materials like iron blocks, red stone, and emerald blocks. Gravel will also become useful and can make a pretty good option from time to time.

Idea #4 – Judge Material Choice by Time and Available Material

The amount of time you have in your hands is a factor every player should consider. Some materials are harder to farm. A good idea for starters is to use the things that are most available. For instance, both oak wood and a lot of birch are usually abundant in many places. You can use them for the meantime while acquiring other materials that are harder to get.

Idea #5 – Just Go Plain Crazy with Your Materials

Of course, you want to go beyond basic protection if you want to make your house look really good. For instance, if you want to give your house that really evil look to keep everyone else at bay, you can add some touches of soul sand or even a good amount of netherrack.

Now if you want to go gung ho in your design, then you might want to do some extreme experimentation and see if you can make a house made of dragon eggs. Feel free to post a video about how you built one.

Idea #6 – Combining Functionality and Good Looks

Many of the suggestions mentioned here will combine both functionality and overall good looks. For instance, you can combine flammable material which may look good and infuse it with tougher and more flame resistant materials like stone in different variants.

Another interesting combination of functionality and thematic overall design is the use of hardened clay. Take note that it has to be colored and also hardened. Whatever house or shelter you build out of it can be made to look really nice, provided that you choose the right blend of colors of course. It also provides a good bit of blast resistance so you can be sure that you're quite safe inside.

Decide on the Roofing

One of the easiest things to spot on any house is the design of the roof. It's literally right up there for the entire world to see. It's also one of the more imaginative aspects of any house design in real life and in Minecraft as well. It may take some practice before people can smoothen out the details on more complex roof designs.

Remember that in this game, roof design is not an exact science. You might think that you have everything planned properly but when you finally implement your layouts, a few things may get awry. That is why everyone is given some sort of creative license to try and fix things that don't go as planned.

The same is true for what people call different roof types and roof designs. Note that some roof templates, types, and designs may look quite similar. This prompts everyone to be a little more cautious about branding and terminology. Some terms may become interchangeable as various styles and designs are implemented in the game. So, be forgiving and give everyone some legroom when words are thrown around.

Idea #7 – Stick to Roofing Basics

If you've been building houses, castles, shelters, cathedrals, and all sorts of stuff in Minecraft then you probably have seen it all. After making all the crazy looking roofs, sometimes going back to the basics may give you a fresh start and think of some new designs to build on.

For instance, you can go back to one of the most basic roof designs in the game, which is the flat roof (see image on the left). You may have constructed this roof a million times over and perhaps you have thought of using it for a fortress design. But have you ever thought of implementing it on a house?

Idea #8 – Flat Roof Leads to Towers

Sometimes going back to these basic designs can give you a refreshing look at things. A flat roof can also hint of adding a tower on one side of the house. In case your house has a nearby village, you can add a bell tower there as a kind of warning for the villagers (just a hint).

If you're the more elusive type and don't really care for villagers or anyone else then you can construct your house with just a plain tower so you can see any incoming. It's also a great defensive structure in case you have to thwart mob efforts.

Some have suggested using some limestone on the top of a flat roof. That has its benefits and drawbacks. For instance, the limestone top will be very easy to spot so your house (or tower if you added one) becomes a beacon for you in case you get lost. That may also become a disadvantage since the same beacon that guides your way also guides others who may have ill intentions, so to speak. It's a double edged sword of a design but it's all up to you if you want to make use of it.

Idea #9 – The Basic Sloped Roof

Another basic roof type is the sloped roof, which is also called as the shed roof. Both terms basically refer to the same thing. The basic sloped roof can be a small challenge to some beginners. For instance, there were those who were starting out who made sloped roofs using cobble.

Idea #10 – Half Steps with Overhangs

Well, the idea of a sloped roof is a good point but when you look at the finished roof something will tell you that it doesn't look exactly right with the house. Sometimes a section will be sticking out especially when you're constructing a roof for a square shaped house. The solution of course is to use half steps with overhangs. That will help to compensate for that stuff during implementation.

Idea #11 – The Terrace: Combining a Sloped and Flat Roof

In case you get tired of either a sloped or flat roof, the next step that everyone usually thinks of is to combine both. One of the easiest ways to combine both roof structures is to create a terrace. Note that there are times when you can implement a terrace and there are times when you can't.

In case your house design allows you to add some flat surface along with your shed roof or sloped roof then a good idea would be to add a terrace with it. Your terrace can be open or if you want shelter from the rain with a lot of open air then add a roof to the thing.

Now, some people call this design a balcony, which is pretty much the same actually. So, if your friend calls it a balcony then just let him call it as it is and you call it a terrace. It doesn't matter since you're referring to one and the same thing but note that there are subtle differences that should be pointed out between a terrace and a balcony.

Idea #12 – Gable Roof

The next roof idea, which is also pretty basic, is the gable roof. It's also a way to make your house look common and inconspicuous. Many village roofs made by the game's terrain generator will have gables on them; which looks like an inverted letter "V." If your house's width is more than 12 blocks then you might want to consider using a gable roof as one of the many designs you can implement.

Idea #13 – Saltbox Roofing

Of course, you may have seen this roofing in real life as well. A saltbox roof looks pretty much like a gable roof, in all respects except that one side of the roof is longer than the other. The longer side may jut downward reaching closer to the floor or it may just be a little more flat and longer on one end but still maintaining the same height as the other side of the roof.

Idea #14 – Clerestory Roof

Simply put, a clerestory roof is one where a window (or windows) is placed at the very top. Well, the window up there isn't for viewing purposes. The main idea behind adding clerestory windows on your roof is to allow more sunlight to come into the building. It's a great way to brighten up the mood inside house especially during the summer days.

Idea #15 – Hip Roof

A hip roof looks like a pyramid that you put on top of your house. Ideally, this roof design is best used for square houses. However, with a little more imagination, you can incorporate hip roofs with other roof details especially if you are building a bigger house or even a manor. An advantage to adding a hip roof to your house is the fact that it allows you to build an attic, a good hiding place in case you're trapped.

Idea #16 – Half Hipped Roof

Creativity knows no bounds and people came up with the half hipped roof. Some people call it the Dutch Gable. However, the Dutch Gable (also known as a gablet roof) has some elements that are unique to it. Nevertheless, some people use these terms interchangeably so be more forgiving.

Idea #17 – Gull Wing

Imagining what a gull wing roof looks like isn't that hard. Just try to imagine a gull trying to fly high up to the sky. The upper section is steeply sloped while the lower section of the roof has a rather shallow pitch. Of course you have to account for the wings that the gull will have on display, which is why gull wing roofs have very wide overhangs on them.

Idea #18 – Dutch Gable

To avoid any arguments, let's call the Dutch Gable as a type of hybrid between the gable and the hipped roof. If you look at it, the gable will usually be on top and the hipped area of the roof will be located on the lower section of the roof. Implementing it in your design can be a little tricky.

Idea #19 – Skillion Roof

The skillion roof looks very much like shed roof. Some people also call skillions as lean-to type of roof. This is because one side of the roof continues to slope onto another roof; sort of leaning on to the roof right next to it. This is the type of roof you will want to use in case you want to add a porch right at the front of the house for that country home theme.

Idea #20 – Gambrel Roof

This is a type of roof where its pitch is divided into two slopes. One slope is designed to be lower than the other. Take note that the slope on a gambrel is located only on one side of the roof.

Idea #21 – Mansard Roof

A mansard looks pretty much like a gambrel. The big difference lies in the fact that the slopes are located on both sides of the roof. It's like you have two sloping sides of gambrels put together.

Idea #22 – North Light Roof

People also call this type of roof as a saw tooth, because if you put one after another, they do look like saw teeth. These are the type of little roofs you can find at the top of factories. They have a series of ridges and they are usually pitched on both sides. The major benefit of course is that it protects the occupants of the house from direct sunlight. Note that all of the windows of the North Light Roof should face either the north or the south.

Idea #23 – Monitor Roofs

You may have seen this type of roof on factories or deeply designed buildings. Some people have used this type of roofing design for log cabins, warehouses, and barns which is pretty interesting to say the least.

A house with a monitor roof looks like it has a smaller house jutting at the top of the ridge of a double pitched roof. It comes complete with clerestory windows and its smaller version of a double pitched roof on top.

Idea #24 – Helm Roof

If you like to do something challenging for a change, then try making a helm roof. It looks like four gable roofs positioned on top of a square house or tower. In case you did incorporate a tower design to house, instead of putting a plain old flat roof on top of the thing, try adding a helm roof to give it a more aesthetic appeal.

Idea #25 – Butterfly or London Roof

If you go around in London, you'll discover that many of the Victorian styled houses have roofs that resemble two inverted letter V's. Some people call them inverted W's but it is really just a matter of choice. In most instances, the main roof of a house will be a basic gable and then a butterfly roof will be incorporated at the edge.

Idea #26 – Thatched Roofs

Here's an idea in case you plan to make some sort of temporary roofing for your shelter. A thatched roof tends to get broken down really fast and it requires some degree of maintenance. This means it isn't what you want for a long-term solution.

Note that the main roofing element is a single flowing layer with no breaks in between. This is to help prevent water from dripping into the house in case it rains. Reeds, straw, or heather are the most common materials that people use to make thatch roofing.

Idea #27 – Conical Roof

You don't usually see conical roofs unless you travel to Asia and find those really ancient buildings and temples. Some Chinese roofs look like these and some houses in and around the Asian nations make use of them too.

Idea #28 – Chinese Roofing

Some people are fascinated about Chinese roofing. Of course, this style of roofing with its concave roof shape isn't a design that is exclusive to the Chinese people. It is in fact a familiar roof shape; you can them also in places like Taipei and Korea. Take note that making these roof designs in Minecraft might require you to a lot of work.

Idea #29 – Stair Blocks

Nothing beats stair blocks. And in case you're just starting out in Minecraft and are looking for the best stuff you can use to make your roof then always go for the basic stair blocks.

It's the simplest way to create your roof without any hassles. Stair blocks already give you that desired steep slope, which is typical for many roofs. Other than that they already look a lot smoother than full blocks so you don't really have to beat around the bush for the details.

Idea #30 – Half Slabs for More Modern Homes

Some people would love to stick to designing more modern homes. This means that they would rather stick to more modern roofing designs. Half slabs look great on modern homes in Minecraft. Of course you'll be using half bricks in order to craft and integrate them into your roof design.

Idea #31 – Add a Spire

It is no secret that castles and towers are very popular in Minecraft. If you love ancient looking brick or stone houses and your design is big enough to include a spire, then add one. You can have that more European turret like spire as an additional defensive feature or you can go for the more aesthetic oriental spire complete with that little dome on top. That will give your house/shelter a more luxurious appeal.

Idea #32 – Domed Shape Roofs

Dome shaped roofs provide your houses with a more Mediterranean theme. You'll be using colored clay for this design. Take note that if you put this type of design right in the middle of woody or medieval European looking neighborhood, your house will stand out.

Dome shapes are welcome and they look very appealing. However, do take note that they are pretty hard to make in Minecraft. So, before you attempt to make one, you better check out some plans and blueprints just to make sure that you're doing things right.

Work on Your House's Interior Design

If you really want to pimp up your house then you better get to work on the interiors. You can say that the real fun happens inside the house. Making the exterior of the house or shelter is a lot of fun but it's not going to be as much fun as making over you house into your very own personalized crib.

If you think that detailing the walls, roof, windows, brick style, lawn, walls/fences, even a little garden is a lot of hard work, wait until you start working on the interiors.

Use a Blueprint to Build Your Interior

Now, there is a lot of planning ahead when you work on your interiors. There are a lot of details that you should pay attention to. In order to make things easier, it is recommended that you use a basic floor plan or blueprint so you will know where each section of the house is and what should go in there.

Interior Elements to Think About

Take note that there are a lot of interior elements that you should really think about. A good way to keep track of what you have already done and what you still need to finish is to create a checklist. Your checklist can be as detailed as you want or as simple as you need it to.

Your basic checklist should include at least some of the following:

- ❖ Electronics
- ❖ Living room stuff

❖ Tables

❖ Bedroom

❖ Kitchen and all the stuff inside it

❖ Bathroom

❖ Bookshelf

❖ Storage facilities

❖ Closets

❖ Cupboards

❖ Fireplaces

❖ Carpets

❖ And pretty much everything else you can add to pimp up your place like chandeliers, torches, glimmering bricks, etc.

Idea #33 – Half Blocks in Bathrooms

Half blocks are useful when making details on your roof. They provide some finer looking tops for your house. However, they also work quite well for your interior. If you use them for your floor, especially where your tub is located then you can at least lower it a bit and it will provide that more realistic effect.

Idea #34 – Black Wool for Gothic Effect

If you love that rather Goth like feel or just want to make things a lot darker inside the house then black wool will make quite an impressive effect. It's a brilliant little thing really. Just patch it up on the walls and voila! You have that nice dark interior which can make you feel like a vampire hiding from the scorching daylight.

Jason Scotts

Idea #35 – Glowstone and Its Many Uses

Glowstone has a lot of applications in this game. You can use them outside the house to help with the visibility at night. Some players even use it at the top of spires and towers to make them more visible at night. They all owe that to the rather "mystical" properties of the glowstone.

If you are constructing a medieval house that incorporates a lot of stone or brick then glowstones make a nice touch if you can't make torches. Make sure to add a sufficient number of glowstone lamps to light the place at night.

Idea #36 – Bookshelves with Your Glowstones

Since we've already covered glowstones, you should know by now that they also provide quite a nice reading light. And yes, the perfect partner to any glowstone lit room is a nice big bookshelf full of hardbound stuff to read. Some players have constructed entire libraries using this great tandem.

Idea #37 – Bathroom Mirror to Add More Character

Bathrooms are not complete without a mirror. That should be a cardinal rule for anyone who makes houses or shelters in this game. In fact, bathroom mirrors should be commonplace even in real life. Use glass, obviously, when making your mirrors. You add character to your bathroom and make things more livable.

Idea #38 – Mirrors to Enhance Space

Sometimes you can't help but be stuck in a small space especially if you have a limited interior space to work with. Try this trick for size – use mirrors (use the big ones!).

Place the mirrors on a wall and it will create the feeling of extra space inside the house. Surprisingly, this works in the game and in real life as well. The glass/mirror will replicate the other side of the house and make the interior look wider than it really is.

Idea #39 – Unconventional Checkerboard Pattern

Checkerboard patterns are in anywhere you go. They add that elegance to any room, whether you're dealing with the bath, living room, or even the bedroom. Now, if you're looking for materials that you can use to make your checkerboard pattern, you will be stuck with a lot of options.

Idea #40 – The Use of Wool

Some materials don't make a totally black color in this game. Some are pretty grayish actually. In case you want to create that really black effect then use wool slabs. In case you decide to make a checkerboard pattern (mentioned in the previous tip), and you can't a practical and really dark color combination then use dark wool and then white stone slabs to get the desired effect.

Idea #41 – Netherbrick and Sandstone for the Bedroom Floor

The bedroom floor should be elegant. It's one place where you can find solace in the game. Using a combination of netherbrick and then sandstone will give your bedroom a more elegant feel.

Idea #42 – Keep Things Simple

Wide open spaces sometimes have a character of their own. That is a good tip both in the game and in real life. If you put in too much detail into your interior then you might end up adding too much clutter for your eyes. Keep things simple and you can find out the true character of your interior design.

Idea #43 – Room Dividers

Another element that needs your attention are room dividers. They can divide the wide expanse of space inside your house like magic. Note that these dividers don't have to be permanent structures. Use wood (especially those that have darker shades to add diffuse some of the brilliance that come from light sources.

Idea #44 – Use Stairs as Dividers

This is a brilliant design idea that you can come across in real life. You may have seen this design in some interior design magazine. A room is divided in the middle using a set of stairs that also lead to the upstairs rooms. One side of the house can be used as the living room while the other half can be used as the kitchen.

Idea #45 – Compartments on the Staircase

Another space saving idea comes in the form of compartments hidden within the staircase. You know that space underneath the stairs that never get used? Well, you can use it as some form of storage space. You can use it as a shelves and storage compartments.

Idea #46 – Thrones for Chairs

It's not every day that you can sit around the house and feel like a king, right? So why not throw a throne right there in your living room? You can design a lazy boy recliner right next to it just to remind you that you're inside your house and not in a castle.

Idea #47 – Stone High Back Chair at the End of a Long Dining Table

If you can't have enough of a power trip, add a long table in your dining room (great if you have the space to use). To complete the effect, add one high back chair at the end, presumably where the master of the house should be seated. Make it out of stone to impose the authority that you want to enshrine.

Idea #48 – Wool for Cushions

Finding cushions in medieval times is a tough job. You can experiment on a lot of materials but nothing really beats wool. White wool looks good as cushions for your chairs especially for your bed. You can make your sheets extra comfy too by making them out of wool.

Idea #49 – Attack of the Minions!

If you can't have enough of the minions from Despicable Me, then add them into your design as well. Use clay that you can color in order to get the desired effect. Make a statue of a minion right beside your fireplace to make that insane cliché effect.

Idea #50 – Maze Type Carpet Design

Carpets can be found on your walls, floors, and just about anywhere inside the house. They can be made out of boring plain colors and designs. Well, here's a thought – why not add a maze in the carpet design. If you get bored after doing all that hard work then you can solve the maze yourself.

Idea #51 – Fireplace in the Outdoors

Let the fireplace be a symbol of your utmost generosity. Not everyone can afford them, or so you may assume. At least the critters outside who want to mob you in the morning can have a place to keep themselves warm. At least you have a way to know where they may be waiting first thing in the morning.

Idea #52 – A Modern Bed in a Medieval Setting

If you want to mess things up a bit then add a modern bed (preferably something that looks like a Tempurpedic). You can show that off to your friends and play with their minds a bit. Make sure to add a headboard, a book, and a night table to complete the desired effect.

Windows

Windows reflect the art in your house. That is of course besides allowing you to have light from the outside world. Other than that, they also allow you to see who's coming in and who's lurking outside your door. Here are some really cool window Ideas:

#53 – Tinted Glass

Tinted glass gives your house a more medieval appeal. They also let you craft some really artsy look. The picture on the left includes some of the colors and shades that you can play with to achieve that ancient effect.

Idea #54 – Stained Glass on Private Chapel

Some people want that rather spiritual effect so they add a mini chapel to their houses. Well, it also helps give you that theme from the middle ages. If you have an altar set up somewhere in the house then you can change one wall to have stained glass pattern on it.

Idea #55 – Stained Glass Panel with Frame on the Garden

If your front lawn or your backyard is pretty secure from damage and mobbing then you may want to accessorize it with free standing glass panel complete with frame balanced on a stone beam. That can even freak out any intruder.

Idea #56 – Secret Window Slots Where You can Fire Your Weapons

Let's face it, sometimes you want to be able to fire at the intruders outside your home. Why not add some secret small window slots with just enough space to fire a weapon. Make it something that you can shut quickly to avoid a counter attack.

Idea #57 – Jalousie Windows

In case you want to stick to something more modern then you can try jalousie windows. It may be a bit of a challenge to build but if you do it, it will be quite an achievement.

Idea #58 – Sash Windows

For those who love the traditional windows from the UK, different variants of sash windows will suffice. You can design either a double hung or a single hung sash.

Idea #59 – Awning Windows

This is a type casement window that swings upward. You can put one of these on your roof to give you access to the top of your house while giving off light from above.

Idea #60 – Emergency Exit/Secret Exit Window

Let's face it, sometimes mobs and all sorts of critters can get in or ruin everything you worked hard for. You don't want to be trapped inside an indefensible shelter. A good idea is to make an emergency exit or even a secret exit window. It should be lower than all other windows and wide enough for you to duck under it.

Chandeliers

These mounted fixtures add light and beauty to your house. You should be making these when everything is already up and running well. They are one of the last things you should add to your house.

Idea #61 – Medieval Wooden Chandelier

If you're just building a nice log house, a wooden chandelier shaped like a cross with glow stones mounted on each end will do nicely. If you have more time in your hands then add candles and make it more intricate than a simple medieval cross.

Idea #62 – Wooden French Empire Chandelier

Wood working is great and wood is something that is easy to get. To get an idea what this chandelier looks like, look for pictures of the White House, specifically of the Red Room.

Idea #63 – Wedding Cake Chandelier

If you want to challenge yourself, then this chandelier with its several tiers will give you enough to chew on.

Idea #64 – Chandelier Made of Bones

Want to scare your visitors? Then grab some bones (+ skulls!) or some other sinister materials you can find from the Nether and make it a chandelier piece.

Miscellaneous, Wacky, and Crazy Ideas

The following are some crazy ideas that don't have a category of their own. Some of these ideas may have come to you in your dreams.

Idea #65 – Igloo

This is one insane idea that will melt away if you use ice. In case you want to make it last, make one out of glass or stone. The shape of the thing can be a bit challenging to craft.

Idea #66 – Trap Doors

Not everyone who steps into you domain is a friend. A trap door, perhaps with spikes underneath, will be a rather interesting welcome.

Idea #67 – Totem Poles

Add totem poles outside of your house (or you can put one inside and use it as a pillar) and let the animal heads freak everyone out. You may want one of the heads to blow fire a la classic Castlevania.

Idea #68 – Pyramid

This will take a long while to build. But if you finish it complete with all the eerie stuff inside, then that will be an awesome achievement you can brag about.

Idea #69 – Hidden Doorways and Mazes

A house full of doors and secret doorways is a maddening maze in itself. Add a door on the top floor that leads to a killer drop. You can also add a maze outside the house to add to the frustration of any attacker.

Idea #70 – Indiana Jones Huge Rolling Rock

Imagine this: People open the front door. All they see is a long hallway. They hear something big crashing from afar. Then they see a huge rock rolling towards them at a killer speed. It's the end for them. Your real entrance is at the secret door under the welcome mat.

Lightning Source UK Ltd.
Milton Keynes UK
UKOW06f0200290414

230766UK00009B/74/P